PAUL JES

RASCAL IN TROUBLE

Illustrated by Bob Lea

A RASCAL STORY

PUFFIN BOOKS

Puffin Books

Published by the Penguin Group (Australia)
250 Camberwell Road
Camberwell, Victoria 3124, Australia
Penguin Books Ltd
80 Strand, London WC2R ORL, England
Penguin Group (USA) Inc.
375 Hudson Street, New York, New York 10014, USA
Penguin Books, a division of Pearson Canada
10 Alcorn Avenue, Toronto, Ontario, Canada, M4V 3B2
Penguin Books (N.Z.) Ltd
Cnr Rosedale and Airborne Roads, Albany, Auckland, New Zealand
Penguin Books (South Africa) (Pty) Ltd
24 Sturdee Avenue, Rosebank, Johannesburg 2196, South Africa
Penguin Books India (P) Ltd
11, Community Centre, Panchsheel Park, New Delhi, 110 017, India

First published by Penguin Books Australia,
a division of Pearson Australia Group Pty Ltd, 2004

1 3 5 7 9 10 8 6 4 2

Text copyright © Lockley Lodge Pty Ltd, 2004
Illustrations copyright © Bob Lea, 2004

Text design by Tony Palmer and Sandy Cull © Penguin Group (Australia)
Cover design by Sandy Cull © Penguin Group (Australia)
Typeset in 14pt Stone Informal by Tony Palmer
Made in Australia by The Australian Book Connection Pty Ltd,
Mt Waverley, Victoria
Film separations by Splitting Image Colour Studio Pty Ltd,
Clayton, Victoria

National Library of Australia
Cataloguing-in-Publication data:

Jennings, Paul, 1943- .
Rascal in trouble.

ISBN 0 14 330037 7.

1. Dragons - Juvenile fiction. I. Lea, Bob, 1952- .
II. Title.

A823.3

www.puffin.com.au

Poor Rascal was outside.

He was cold.

Bomber was warm and snug inside.
So were Shovel, Sniff and Ruff-Ruff.

Sherry let them all sleep inside
whenever they liked.

'Please let Rascal in,' said Ben.

'Sherry lets her dragons in.'

'Teach Rascal to beg,' said Dad.
'Then he can come in.'

'Beg, Rascal,' said Ben. 'Then you
can come inside.'

But Rascal did not beg. He unlocked
the door with his tail.

And ran inside.

'Out you go,' said Dad. 'You are
not coming in until you beg.'

'Beg, Rascal,' said Ben. 'Like this.'

But Rascal did not beg. He unlocked
the window with his tail.

Rascal jumped inside.

'Out you go,' said Dad. 'You are
not coming in until you beg.'

'You have to beg, Rascal,' said Dad.

'Then you can come inside.'

But Rascal did not beg.

He climbed into the chimney.

And jumped out of the fireplace.

Dad was not happy.

'This is your last chance, Rascal,'
said Dad. 'You have to beg.'

Just then, the wind blew
the door shut.

They were locked out.

The key was inside.

'Please open the door with your tail, Rascal,' said Dad. 'It's cold out here.'

'Beg, Dad,' said Ben. 'You have
to beg.'

'Please open the door, Rascal,'
begged Dad.

So the little dragon put his tail
in the lock and opened the door.

After that, Rascal stayed inside
whenever he liked.

He was warm and snug all the time.

But he didn't beg. Not ever.